"Well I never! Oh my goodness!" said the Admirable, when he had read the letter.

"What does it say, Bapu?" asked Ravi.

"I shall have to get busy at once," said the Admirable. He opened the front door, picked up a tin of polish and started rubbing the doorstep. Ravi picked up the letter and read it.

"A competition!" he shouted. "For the most beautiful lock on the canal! We'll win, Bapu, I'm sure we will!"

Admirable Karia went into the garden.

"Now then, number one grandson," he said. "We must get started. First, inspection of premises. Second, planning of improvements. Third, carrying out operations. Fourth …"

"Winning the prize, Bapu," interrupted Ravi.

"Quite right. Now let's start the inspection."

THE LOCK COMPETITION

Story by Mary Risk

illustrations by The County Studio

HEINEMANN · LONDON

One morning, Admirable Karia was polishing his telescope. He opened the window and looked along the canal.

"Smoke!" he said. "And there's no smoke without fire. What a calamity!" He put the telescope down, and looked out again.

"Most peculiar. The smoke's gone!"

He scratched his head, and thought. Then he looked at the end of the telescope, and laughed. "Dust on the glass!" he said. "What an old duffer I am!"

The letterbox rattled.

"Aha," said the Admirable. "The postman."

He hurried downstairs. A letter lay on the doormat. Admirable Karia picked it up and turned it over and over.

"Hm. Postmark Grimspool. I wonder now. Is it a bill? Oh dear. Very worrisome. Very awkward, owing to poor financial situation. Or is it from a friend? Who do I know in Grimspool?"

There was a thumping, clattering noise behind him. Ravi was jumping down the stairs two at a time.

"Hello, Bapu," he said. "You've got a letter."

"Yes," said the Admirable. "But I don't know who it's from."

"Why don't you open it and see?"

"Eh? What? Good idea. Young minds work faster than old ones every time. Now, let me see …"

"Disorder in the rose department," said the Admirable. "Disgraceful behaviour of the hollyhocks. Also, the grass needs cutting." He shook his head. "Very difficult, with my old mower."

"And shouldn't we paint the door?" said Ravi. "It's all chipped."

"Certainly. And the windows need a wash. What a lot to do!"

From up the canal came a sharp 'toot, toot'.

"Here comes Joshua Jones with the *Delilah*," said the Admirable. "He's picking up a delivery for Biggott's Wharf."

Ravi started thinking. Biggott's Wharf – Fiona Cashmore – the Cashmore's flat – window boxes …

"Bapu!" he said suddenly. "Can I go to Biggott's with Josh? I've had a brilliant idea."

The *Delilah* arrived and Josh jumped out.

"Remarkable news arrived this morning," said the Admirable. "There's going to be a ..."

"Beautiful Lock Competition!" interrupted Ravi.

"Well I never," said Josh. "Whose idea is this?"

"Mr Biggott's," said the Admirable.

"Good for him," said Josh. "He takes a pride in this canal, he does."

It didn't take long for Josh and Ravi to chug up to Biggott's Wharf.

"Thanks for the lift," said Ravi as he jumped ashore.

Ravi hurried off. He met Fiona coming out of the Cashmore's flat.

"You'll never guess what's going to happen," he said.

"You mean the Beautiful Lock Competition?" said Fiona. "Mr Biggott told Daddy this morning. Ravi, we've *got* to win it!"

"We will," said Ravi. "Listen, I've had an idea. Do you remember those extra window boxes your dad bought last year? He never used them, did he?"

"No. We could fill them with flowers and put them along the lock wall. Brilliant, Ravi! Let's go and ask him."

Wilton Cashmore wasn't in the flat. He wasn't in the office, either. Someone else was though. Spanner was sitting with his feet up, eating a chocolate bar.

"Where's Daddy?" asked Fiona.

"Don't ask me," said Spanner. "Nobody tells me anything."

Wilton marched in. His arms were full of plants.

"Spanner!" he barked. "What are you doing?"

"Just finishing my elevenses, Mr Cashmore," said Spanner.

"Daddy," said Fiona, "can I have those old window boxes please? The ones you never used? We want them for the lock wall."

"You can't do that, pet," said Wilton. "The lock wall must be kept clear. And anyway, I need them here. Mr Biggott wants the wharf to look beautiful too. Take that pot of paint. That should smarten things up a bit."

"Where's Bapu?" said Ravi when he and Fiona arrived back at Lock Cottage.

A head popped up from behind the flowers.

"Making all shipshape," said the Admirable. "Now it's all hands on deck. Ravi, clean the windows. Elbow grease, that's what we need. Fiona, kindly sweep the paths. All unruly weeds must be ruthlessly dealt with."

They worked hard all day.

"Are these windows all right now, Bapu?" said Ravi.

"A splendid job. Bright enough for a lighthouse."

"Will these paths do, Admirable?" asked Fiona.

"First class work. You are promoted to first mate. In fact, I shall issue extra rations all round."

"Do you mean it's tea-time?" said Ravi. "I'm starving."

The next day, Fiona arrived at the lock early.

"Come on, Ravi," she said. "There's still a lot to do."

"Like what?"

"We haven't painted the door yet. I've brought some brushes. We can use the paint Daddy gave us."

Ravi fetched the tin and opened it.

The paint was a brilliant sky blue.

"What a horrible colour," said Ravi.

"Most unfortunate," said the Admirable.

"Daddy must have given me the wrong tin," said Fiona. "This is the paint he got by mistake for my room, and never used."

"Don't worry, first mate," said the Admirable. "We'll give the door a jolly good wash. Now, what's that terrible noise?"

A motorbike screeched to a halt outside Lock Cottage.

"Spanner!" said Ravi. "Where did you get that bike?"

"It's on trial," said Spanner grandly. "I'm thinking of buying it."

"But you haven't got any money," said Fiona.

"So what?" said Spanner. "No harm in thinking, is there?"

He held up a tin of paint.

"This is from Sharon. She thought it might come in handy. Nice colour, too. Look." He opened the tin for them.

"Pink. Er ... well ..." said Ravi.

"Cooee!" Sharon was calling to them from the Delilah.

"Hello, Shar," said Spanner. "You're here early."

"I closed the cafe and came with Josh. I thought I'd better soak up a bit of the atmosphere beforehand. I'm official photographer for the competition – great, eh?" she added proudly.

"What's all this then?" asked Josh looking at the tins of paint.

"The front door's all chipped and we want to repaint it. But Daddy's paint is horrible, and Sharon's is even worse," said Fiona.

"Hey, steady on!" said Sharon. "I've got taste, I have. Spanner says so."

"I don't think you've too much of a problem there," said Josh. "Admirable, could you find me an old bucket?"

Josh poured a splodge of blue and then a splodge of pink into the bottom of the bucket. It made a lovely purple colour.

"Most attractive," said the Admirable. "An excellent match with the flowers."

"I'll mix it all up then," said Josh.

"Lovely!" said everyone when it was ready.

"Off you go, then!" said Josh. "See you later – I'm going for forty winks on the Delilah."

"Give the rest of that paint here," said Spanner, when Ravi and Fiona had finished painting the door. "I'll splosh it round the windows."

"No sploshing, please," said the Admirable firmly. "Windows to stay white, thank you very much."

"Can we paint the bollards, Bapu?" said Ravi.

"Good idea. They'll have time to dry before the judge arrives."

"Ooh heck," said Spanner, "I'd better be getting back to the wharf. I don't want Mr Cashmore catching me down here."

"Why is Daddy coming here?" asked Fiona.

"Don't you know?" replied Spanner. "Mr Biggott's judging the competition, and your Dad's bringing him in his car."

Soon everything was nearly ready.

"Just the tricky bits near the ground now," said Fiona.

"Grass finished," panted the Admirable, putting away his heavy old lawnmower.

They all stood back and admired their handiwork.

"Oh no!" groaned Ravi. "Look at the lifebelt! It's all old and
stained. We'll never clean it up in time."

An impatient horn blared nearby.

"That'll be Daddy and Mr Biggott," said Fiona. "They must be
stuck behind something. It's probably Joe Laski's tractor."

"A last minute hitch," muttered the Admirable. "Most
annoying!"

"I know," said Ravi, jumping up and down. "Josh can lend us his lifebelt."

"Hurry, Ravi!" said Fiona.

"Run up the lane, Fiona," said the Admirable, "and ask Mr Laski to go *very* slowly. Hold Mr Cashmore up for a moment or two."

Ravi heard Fiona call to Joe Laski. Then he heard the tractor change to a lower gear.

He sped down the path and rapped on the cabin roof.

"Josh, Josh quickly!"

"What's the emergency?" asked Josh. "Fire? Man overboard?"

Ravi explained, and the lifebelts were swapped in no time.

Sharon had appeared from behind a hedge.

"It's so peaceful in the countryside," she said. "Us artistic types appreciate the beauties of nature you know."

"What about this beauty then?" said Josh, pointing to the Lock Cottage. The lifebelt was in position and everything looked perfect.

"Oo, I say," said Sharon. "Looks a treat, it does. I still think it's a funny colour on that door though," she added, winking at Josh.

With a last impatient honk, Wilton's car drew up. He got out of the driving seat and opened the door behind.

"Would you like to step this way, Mr Biggott?" he said.

A week later, Admirable Karia was polishing his telescope again. Fiona and Ravi were watching him.

"Can I look, Bapu?" said Ravi. "I want to see if Josh is coming. He said we'd have the result today." He looked down the telescope.

"Yes! He's coming! Let's go and meet him!"

Five minutes later, the *Delilah* arrived. Josh threw the newspaper to Fiona.

"Read all about it!" he said.

"'First prize to Lock Cottage!'" read Fiona. "'Mr Biggott awards a generous prize of £100 to Mr A. Karia. 'We must all work hard to preserve our beautiful canal,' the famous magnate says.'"

"But that's not Mr Biggott in the photograph," said Ravi.

"No, it's Daddy," said Fiona. "He must have got in front by accident when Sharon was taking the photograph."

"A hundred pounds!" said the Admirable, beaming from ear to ear. "A hundred pounds! A new lawnmower at last!"

William Heinemann Ltd. Michelin House,
81 Fulham Road, London SW3 6RB

LONDON MELBOURNE AUCKLAND

First published 1992 by William Heinemann Ltd
Joshua Jones film copyright © 1990 S4C
Joshua Jones character copyright © 1989 Rob Lee
Text copyright © 1992 William Heinemann Ltd
Illustrations copyright © 1992 William Heinemann Ltd
All rights reserved
Based on the animation series produced by
Bumper Films for S4C – Channel 4 Wales –
and Prism Art & Design Ltd

ISBN 434 96224 4

Printed and bound in Italy
by OFSA - Milano